SPOOK SPOTTING

When ace spook-spotter Amy goes to stay in an old castle with her best friend Hannah, a high-spirited adventure is guaranteed!

Mary Hooper knows what makes a good story – she's had over six hundred published in teenage and women's magazines and she's also a fiction reader for IPC magazines. In addition, she's the highly-regarded author of over twenty titles for young people, including the Walker titles *Best Friends, Worst Luck* and *The Boyfriend Trap*. She's married with two "nearly grown-up" children.

Some other titles

The Green Kids
by Sam McBratney

Haddock 'n' Chips
by Linda Hoy

Jackson's Juniors
by Vivian French

Jim's Winter
by Kathy Henderson

Kachunka!
by Enid Richemont

*The Mystery of the
Rugglesmoor Dinosaur*
by Alison Leonard

Titch Johnson
by Mark Haddon

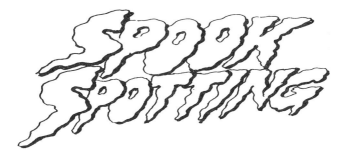

MARY HOOPER

Illustrations by

SUSAN HELLARD

WALKER BOOKS
AND SUBSIDIARIES

LONDON • BOSTON • SYDNEY

First published 1993 by Walker Books Ltd
87 Vauxhall Walk, London SE11 5HJ

This edition published 1994

2 4 6 8 10 9 7 5 3

This book has been typeset in Plantin.

Printed in England

British Library Cataloguing in Publication Data
A catalogue record for this book is
available from the British Library.

ISBN 0-7445-3184-5

Contents

Chapter One 7

Chapter Two 17

Chapter Three 27

Chapter Four 37

Chapter Five 49

Chapter Six 59

Chapter Seven 69

Chapter Eight 81

Chapter One

I heard Hannah pounding back upstairs two steps at a time, but I didn't dare stop reading. It was *Spooks and Superghosts* and I was just coming to the good bit – the bit where the massively horrible fiend from the lake enters the abbey and meets the ghost of the long-dead knight on horseback. I'd read it before, of course, so I knew what was going to happen, but it was still really exciting.

Hannah burst into the bedroom. "Guess what!" she said.

Well, I didn't think it was anything much – she'd only gone downstairs to tell her mum that she'd seen a lesser spotted something-or-other flying past. Hannah was a bird-watcher, you see; I ought to mention that straight away.

I rolled my eyes. "Bet it's just that you've seen some daft old bird in the garden," I said.

"No, it's better than that. Put that silly spook book down, Amy, and guess properly."

It was Saturday – the Saturday before half-term week. We were round at Hannah's house and her mum was going to take us to the cinema that afternoon. I wanted to see *Adventure at Craghill Spar* ("A riveting real-life story of how two brave children foil a malicious medieval spirit and return a kingdom to its rightful owner" – I'd already read the book) and Hannah wanted to see some nature film about a bird and a dog walking across a desert.

Grudgingly, keeping my finger on the line I was on, I put my book down and looked up at her. "A golden eagle just swooped down and carried off the cat?"

"Don't be stupid," she said, "you don't get golden eagles round here." She stationed herself back by the window – she'd been there most of the morning. "But I do have to keep looking out, because the wind's blowing from the east and I'm sure we're going to see some sea birds. Maybe a kittiwake will go by. I mean, I know we're some distance from..."

I went back to *Spooks and Superghosts*. The only thing that worried me was that the long-departed knight on horseback had to come out of a concealed cupboard place where he'd been boarded up for a couple of hundred years, and in the illustration the cupboard plainly wasn't even big enough for the knight, let alone a horse in full armour.

"Of course, with sea birds…" Hannah was saying, and then she stopped. "Amy! You haven't guessed."

"Give up," I mumbled, anxious to get back to the knight.

"Well," she said tantalizingly. "My dad just said he's got to go to Wales on business all next week … and if we like he'll take us to stay with my gran and gramps – they live on the way!"

I put down *Spooks and Superghosts*. "Really?" I said.

"All on our own!" Hannah gloated. "No mums or dads!"

Well, I'd never met Hannah's gran and grandad, but the thought of staying anywhere on our own was exciting. So far, the only place I'd been without Mum was the school's country farm. Great, I'd thought then, freedom – but there had been so many teachers and minders that if you so much as blew your nose three of them asked you if you were coming down with a cold.

"They're all right, Gran and Gramps," said Hannah. "They'll be busy, mind, because it's the last week that the castle's open to the public this season and…"

"*Castle!*" I squealed.

"Yes, castle," she said calmly, just as if she was telling me that they had a sub post office. "They don't own it, of course. They're just tenants for the National Trust. House-keepers."

"But … but … housekeepers in a *castle*!"

She nodded again. "It's not that big, you know. Old, but not big. A fortified manor house, they call it."

"Oh, wow!" I said, while knights in armour, princesses leaning out of towers, ghosts with their heads under their arms, and dreadful horrid fiends jostled in my head for attention. "But... I mean – is it a *real* castle? Is it *haunted*?"

"Haunted?" she said. "I shouldn't think so. Gran wouldn't hold with anything like that."

"But ... are there vampires in the spare rooms and do you wake in the night to the sound of chains rattling? When you open cupboards do skeletons fall out and will there be priests' holes in the walls? And—"

"Of course not," Hannah said, screwing up her face in disgust. "But what is exciting is that a part of the grounds is kept as a wildlife sanctuary, so there should be some pretty rare birds around. Of course, they won't be nesting at this time of year, but I just bet I see some good ones."

"I bet..." I breathed. Before *Spooks and Superghosts*, I'd been reading a book where a girl had gone to a castle, found an old mirror, and through it had travelled back in time. While in the sixteenth century she'd saved a witch's life (only she wasn't really a witch, just an old woman who made potions out of herbs) and been given some treasure in return. She'd left the treasure behind when she'd gone back to the twentieth century, but she'd remembered where she'd hidden it, and found it again in time to save the life of her little brother (Simon, called Sine), who needed a very expensive operation. *A Witch in Time Saves Sine* it was called. Great, it was.

"Er … are there any big mirrors in the castle?" I asked Hannah. "Any really old ones which go all misty when you look into them?"

"Don't think so," she said.

I was disappointed, but got over it. "Bet you wouldn't notice a mysterious old mirror anyway, not unless it had a robin perched on it."

"I might not even notice it then," said Hannah. "Robins aren't exactly head turning, are they? I might notice if it was a corn bunting or a long-eared owl."

I giggled, and then I thought, well, there were bound to be some mirrors in the castle –

it was just up to me to find the right one. *And* find the priests' holes and half-dead vampires and mysterious, wailing maidens who were there one minute and vanished into mist the next.

"I'm going to discover some spooks!" I said to Hannah. "I'm going to find secret rooms and … and walled-up skeletons and ghostly, walking monks." I remembered a programme I'd seen on TV about a girl who was always having spooky things happen to her. "I'm going to be world famous for discovering them. I'm going to be on television!"

"Oh, right," said Hannah. "I take it you want to come, then."

"Try and stop me!" I said.

Chapter Two

"Now, are you sure you've got everything?" Mum said as we waited for Hannah and her dad to collect me.

"No, I'm not sure," I said crossly. She'd taken out all the specially useful items I'd got together. I'd made myself a stake, for instance – just a small one, easily packed, to put through a vampire's heart – and she'd taken it out, saying what on earth did I want a ruler, pointed at one end, for. She'd also taken out a candle (they always have candles in the books – when the flame flickers and goes out, you know there's a ghostly presence nearby). And she'd taken out the chisel I'd been going to use to open cupboards that had been closed for thousands of years.

All I had left were boring things: jumpers and vests and pants. When the adventures happened I was going to be severely under-equipped.

"Now, Hannah's gran and grandad are going to be very busy, Amy," Mum said. "So you won't keep bothering them, will you?"

"Of course not," I said. I would be a model visitor, quietly amusing myself around the castle and grounds – and just as I was leaving I'd present them with the casket of treasure I'd found in the strange and mysterious sealed-up room I'd discovered when I'd counted the number of windows outside and realized there was one too many.

"And give Hannah's gran these flowers straight away," Mum said, looking doubtfully at the bunch she held. She'd gone down to the market as soon as I'd arrived back from Hannah's yesterday, but there had only been one stall still open, with all its flowers half price. When you saw them you knew why.

"Perhaps you could say something about falling on them on the way down," Mum said worriedly, picking brown bits off.

"They're not so much squashed as dead," I said.

"Well, falling on them might have killed them," said Mum. "Anyway, say how kind it is of her gran and grandad to have you – and don't start being fussy about your food; you just eat and drink everything you're given."

"Everything?" I said darkly. "What if a mysterious enchanter tries to make me drink deadly poison from a silver chalice?"

Mum tutted. "Those books of yours!" she said. "You just make sure you keep warm. Layers is the answer in a cold house. A vest and a T-shirt and a shirt and a jumper."

"I won't be able to move..."

"Never mind," Mum said, "at least you'll be warm. Oh, and if they offer you a hot-water bottle make sure the stopper..."

I darted off to the kitchen. I'd suddenly remembered something vitally important. It was her talking about being cold that had made me remember. Cold ... tombstones ... vampires ... *garlic!* Everyone knew that you only had to show Dracula some garlic and he immediately crumbled into dust. I *had* to have garlic if I had nothing else. It was vital.

I opened our big kitchen cupboard and stared in. The thing was, I wasn't sure what

sort of garlic it should be. Garlic salt? Maybe
you sort of sprinkled it over him. Garlic
mayonnaise? No, surely not; he'd never stand
still long enough for you to smear it on. I
yanked open the fridge door; what about
garlic and mushroom pizza that you could
throw at him like a Frisbee?

"What are you doing now?" Mum's voice
came from the hall. "Hannah's dad is just
pulling up outside."

"Coming!" I said, frantically shuffling
around packets of garlic-and-herb stuffing
mix, garlic butter and garlic flavoured crisps.
My eyes fell on the string of garlic hanging by
the back door. Of course! A whole bulb of
garlic; the real thing.

But what do you do with it? I wondered.
Would you peel off cloves and chuck them at
your vampire one by one? Or roll the whole
thing across the floor to try and trip him up?
I reached for the kitchen scissors and cut
myself a bulb. Never mind. When the time
came I'd know instinctively. They always

did in the books.

There was a ring on the bell and Mum opened the door.

"Ready?" said Hannah, darting into the kitchen to find me.

"You bet," I said. "Got your bird books?"

"Course! And I've borrowed an amazing pair of binoculars from the man next door *and* I've got some camouflage gear."

"Come on then, you two," Mum said, coming into the kitchen with the flowers behind her back. "It's a long journey and Hannah's dad will want to be off."

"We'll see you next Friday, Mrs Davies," Hannah said.

"Behave yourselves, won't you, and help with the washing-up and – what on earth's that?" Mum, who'd been patting my arm in a motherly way, suddenly found herself patting a bulb of garlic. "What's that big lump under your jumper, Amy?"

"Just a … a something to play with on the journey," I lied.

Hannah, by now, was lugging my case to the car. I picked up a torch from the hall table and followed her down the path. Mum followed, poking me in the garlic.

"Morning, Mrs Davies," said Hannah's dad, standing at the car boot ready to put my case away.

Mum had to stop poking and look all pleasant and grateful. "This is so nice of you!" she said, pleasantly and gratefully. "Are you sure Hannah's gran won't mind having them?"

"She'll love it!" Hannah's dad said.

Mum brought out the flowers from behind her back, the lump on my arm forgotten. "Amy got her some flowers. They're a bit bedraggled, I'm afraid, and the journey won't help, but…" Desperate to get rid of the flowers, she pushed them at me. "In you get, Amy. Be good! See you both next Friday!"

I waved at Mum all the way down the road. Six days in a castle; anything could happen. When I saw her again I might not be *me* – I might have been taken over by a mysterious spirit from another time zone. Or maybe it would have been discovered (through a strangely-shaped birthmark on my leg) that I was actually a princess who'd been lost to the world.

Hannah, next to me in the back, nudged me excitedly and passed me a butterscotch. "Can't wait!" she said. "I wonder if I'll see a white-fronted goose…"

"Or, even better, a white-fronted *ghost*!" I said.

Chapter Three

My first sight of the castle was a good and spooky one. We'd been driving for hours and hours (with a stop at a motorway café for bacon sandwiches) and had just gone over an almost-mountain, when Hannah started getting quite excited, saying we were nearly there and talking about yellowhammers and collared doves and things.

We went over another small hill and round a sharp bend in the road.

"Just round the next corner!" Hannah said and my stomach lurched with excitement. Suddenly, there it was: Murdo Castle, sitting in a valley with a wispy bit of mist wrapped intriguingly round it. It wasn't a Cinderella type of castle – it didn't have turrets or glittering spires – and it wasn't a Sleeping Beauty rambling-and-ruined type, either. It was a solid, forbidding sort of castle, I thought, and felt a fearful shiver of anticipation. There was a garden with lots of clipped hedges in the front, and a lake to one side, and then just behind was a dark, brooding wood, which was the bird sanctuary place, I supposed.

The castle itself was a grey stone, two-storey, long and flatish sort of building with proper castle up-and-down bits all along the top and a flag flying in the middle, above the big doorway. The gravelled car park in front was crowded ("Tourists," said Hannah's dad dismissively) and to the right was a newish bookshop and small café. The mist, disappointingly, had disappeared once we were close.

There were various signs saying VISITORS THIS WAY, PLEASE WAIT FOR THE NEXT GUIDED TOUR and PLEASE SHOW YOUR TICKET, but Hannah's dad led us straight round to the back and past another sign saying STRICTLY PRIVATE.

"Gran and Gramps have got their own little apartment in the north wing," Hannah explained.

"They don't live in the whole castle, then?"

"How could they, silly. How could two of

them live in thirty-eight rooms?"

"Thirty-eight rooms," I repeated. That was without the mysterious forgotten one which I was going to discover. It would be a thirty-nine roomed castle by the time I went home. They'd have to change all the guide books.

"They'd *rattle* in all those rooms, wouldn't they?" Hannah went on. "And think of the heating costs in winter!"

"S'pose so," I said absent-mindedly, and then my eyes fell on a witch's broom propped up outside a shed in the cobbled yard. I gawped at it – a proper witch's broom, just standing there as casually as anything.

I put out a shaking hand and pointed. "L–look!" I whispered to Hannah. "A witch has probably just got off it and is inside the castle now, mixing dead things into a stew in a cauldron."

"My gran wouldn't let her – she won't even let me make fudge," Hannah said.

Hannah's dad looked over his shoulder and grinned. "Quaint, isn't it? A proper country broom; they're called besoms. The gardener here makes them himself out of hazel twigs."

"Oh," I said. And then I thought, well, maybe the gardener was an evil wizard. I'd have to get him to stand in front of a mirror and see if he had a reflection. If he didn't, then that would prove it. Or was it Dracula who didn't have a reflection?

"Come in, my loves!" Hannah's gran was hurrying across the kitchen to welcome us. It was quite an ordinary, modern kitchen – no cauldrons, no copper things hanging up or spikes going round and round with an ox cooking on them.

"Have you had a good journey?" she asked. She was another slight disappointment. Well, wouldn't you think that a gran who lived in a castle would be very tall and thin, with a cackly voice? A bit like Cinderella's wicked stepmother? This gran wasn't. She was quite tall, but she was wearing a smart suit and high heels and had slightly blue hair and two rows of pearls.

Hannah's dad introduced me, and her gran said she was delighted to have me there and I was to call them Gran and Gramps, just as Hannah did.

"You're very much alike," she said, looking from one of us to the other. "Same size, same colouring."

We were, actually – teachers remarked on it. In fact, when we'd just decided to be best friends and go round together I had wondered if perhaps she and I were twins, stolen by goblins and separated at birth. Mum had roared with laughter when I'd mentioned it, though. And so had Hannah, come to that.

"And are you alike in other ways?"

Hannah and I both shook our heads. "Not a bird fan then, Amy?" Gran asked.

Hannah grinned. "Amy reads spooky adventure books," she said. "She's a bookworm."

"So you must be a birdworm," I said, and everyone laughed.

"Now, you two make yourselves at home," said Gran. "Gramps is in the entrance hall taking the money at the moment, but you'll meet him later."

I remembered to say how nice it was of her to have me, and handed over the flowers, which looked a lot worse.

"Sorry they're a bit brown," I said. "I fell on them in the car."

Hannah nudged me because they'd actually been in the boot all the way.

"How charming!" Gran said. As she took the soggy bunch two heads fell off and we both pretended not to notice. "Now, you can show Amy round, Hannah, but you won't be able to go into all the rooms right now because the public are evcrywhere."

"That's OK, Gran!" Hannah said. "We'll start with the wood. Can't wait to see if you've still got any summer visitors…"

Hannah got her notebook out of the car and, while her dad sat down with Gran and had a cup of tea, off we went.

On the cover of Hannah's notebook it said, *Birds spotted: Murdo Castle, October 12th – 17th.* I had a notebook, too, and on the cover of mine I'd written, *Spooky and mysterious happenings spotted: Murdo Castle, October 12th – 17th.*

We went into the wood (a notice said PLEASE RESPECT THE PRIVACY OF OUR FEATHERED FRIENDS) and Hannah stopped to write. I looked over her shoulder and read, *Time: 3.28 p.m. First observations in wood.*

I wrote in *my* notebook (very tidily, because the TV company who'd make the documentary about me would want to use it as evidence), *Time: 3.28 p.m. First observations of castle. Extremely spooky. Mist hanging about in mist-erious way. Witch's broom outside back door. Note: remember to check on gardener.*

Chapter Four

We went through the wood, bumping into tourists and trying to look important and as if we lived there, and while Hannah looked at birds and their tracks and picked up the occasional feather, I observed the castle from all angles.

By the time we went back (and Hannah had made two pages of notes) her dad was just leaving. He gave us the standard talk about being good and helping, and we went out to the drive to wave him off. By this time all the visitors were leaving, too, and I felt pleasantly important because we were still there, obviously not *ordinary* girls. I expect they thought we were princesses who lived there all the time.

I was desperate to look round and start having adventures and seeing ghosts, but there were still official-looking people in some of the rooms so I couldn't have a really good poke about. Anyway, before we'd got very far, Gran came to find us to tell us supper was ready.

"We're eating in our own little kitchen in the north wing, of course," she said; but she told Hannah to show me the dining hall on the way.

It was enormous. There was a gallery at the top ("Where minstrels sang to the Lord and Lady," Hannah said) and paintings and tapestry hangings on the walls. The long wooden table was laid with masses of cutlery and china and glasses and silver dishes and candles. In each corner of the room was a vast flower arrangement on a stand. It looked great.

"All it needs," I said in an awe-struck whisper to Hannah, "is the ghost of a knight on horseback standing near the fireplace."

"Daft!"

I gave a little scream. Just by the door was a suit of armour. "Look!" I said. "I bet there's a skeleton still inside!"

Hannah tutted, but I went to look.

"Can't get the visor up!" I said, standing on tiptoe to reach. I rattled and pushed and suddenly it shot open, squashing one of my fingers.

"Ow!" I cried.

"Skeleton bite you?" Hannah said.

"They must have taken him out earlier," I mumbled, sucking the finger.

I shot another look round the room. Masses of wooden panelling! I had to come back here on my own; I knew if I just tapped the right panel a whole section of wall would slide away, revealing a mysterious cobweb-lined tunnel leading to a crypt. I wasn't quite sure what a crypt was, actually, but spooky places always had them.

"Come on!" Hannah said. "Gramps will be waiting."

Gramps was another severe disappointment – not a swirling black cloak or a magic wand in sight, just a lot of white hair and a moustache which he twiddled. He seemed nice enough, though, and after supper took me into their hall so I could ring Mum and let her know I'd arrived safely.

"What's it like, then?" Mum asked.

"Dead exciting!" I said, and told her about the witch's broom and the panelled room and the disappearing mist and everything.

"And did you give Hannah's gran the flowers?"

"Yes, yes," I said impatiently.

"Was she pleased with them? Has she put them in a vase somewhere?"

I thought of the hugely ornate flower arrangements in the dining hall. If she'd put them anywhere, she'd probably put them in the dustbin. "Oh, yes," I lied.

"There's not much in the garden at this time of the year. I expect she'll be glad of a bit of colour," Mum said, and I just grunted.

After Hannah had phoned home we watched some TV but Hannah kept yawning, so Gran said she'd show us up to our room. "I suggest you have an early night tonight and explore properly tomorrow," she said, leading us upstairs. "Tomorrow we're shut – no more visitors until Tuesday."

Well, I didn't mind going to bed – I had more things to write in my notebook.

"Hannah usually has our little spare room, but it's not big enough for two," Gran said, leading us along a dark corridor. "I've put you both in the blue room in the main part of the castle."

"Great!" Hannah said. She nudged me. "You'll like it in there."

"I've made up the bed and put an electric blanket on, so I don't think you'll be cold," Gran continued, stopping in front of a heavy wooden door. "But if you are, there are more blankets in the big chest."

Big chest! Of course there would be a secret compartment at the bottom. Or a puzzling clue – one old shoe, or half a letter written in blood by a vampire. I felt for my trusty garlic bulb, still stuffed up my jumper sleeve.

Gran pushed open the door and switched on the light. The room was huge with great, heavy blue curtains with fringes and traily bits and – oh, wow! – it had a four-poster bed!

Gran smiled. "It's two hundred years old," she said.

"And was it slept in by Elizabeth the First?" I asked breathlessly.

"Not quite, but if you like you can pretend it was."

She left us and Hannah started unpacking while I stalked round the bed, examining it minutely.

"Now, we've got to be careful," I said. "I once read a book where what looked like a perfectly ordinary four-poster bed was actually a trap. Someone went to sleep in it and when they woke up – well, they never did wake up – the top of the bed had come down on top of them, squashing them to death."

"Just fancy," Hannah said, pulling on her pyjamas.

"And then in another book, two friends pulled the curtains all round the four-poster and in the morning, when they opened them, they had mysteriously slipped into another time. They were back in Victorian days."

"Hm," Hannah said. "If that happens it'll be very interesting to see what birds are around."

"You can laugh," I said darkly, "but you wouldn't like it really. S'pose you were in Victorian times and you had to climb chimneys and things. And wear bustles and those silly bonnets."

We went into the bathroom, which was next door. It was freezing, white-tiled and old-fashioned. I cautioned Hannah about turning on the tap, saying that I wouldn't be at all surprised if – I gave a horrid chuckle here – blood came out, but she just turned it on anyway and it was perfectly all right.

We went back to our room and, after making sure that the ceiling of the bed wasn't going to come down on us, climbed in.

I wrote in my notebook, *Suit of armour in dining hall – skeleton already removed. Must investigate panelling – find sliding wall to crypt as soon as possible. Four-poster bed – doesn't seem to have squashing mechanism.*

As neither of us could stop yawning by then, we decided to go to sleep.

"See you in the morning if we haven't been squashed," Hannah said.

"And if we're both in the same time zone," I added.

She turned off the bedside lamp and I lay in the darkness for a while, listening to the ghostly noises of an owl in the distance. An owl – or it might have been a soul in torment.

I turned over, moved closer to Hannah and gave a little scream. There was an unearthly glowing light and it was creeping across the floor. At any moment we could be attacked by a red blob that turned itself into a fire serpent when it reached us!

"H–h–" I croaked, the word sticking in my throat through sheer terror. If the serpent swallowed us up I'd never get on TV. At this thought I managed a wavery "Help!" and shook Hannah.

"What now?" she asked. "Don't tell me, the bed's been taken over by a creature from beyond the grave."

"No! Look!" I said, pointing to the glowing light.

"That's just the switch of the electric blanket," said Hannah. "Turn it off before we go to sleep, will you?"

Chapter Five

When we woke up in the morning we were still there. We hadn't been squashed or transported to another time zone, and I didn't know whether to be pleased or disappointed.

"I'm putting on my camouflage gear," Hannah said, struggling into a sort of beige and greeny-coloured thing. "The birds won't see me in this."

"And I'm putting on my sorting-out-spooks gear," I said, putting on my jeans and tucking my garlic up my sleeve.

"I'll see you downstairs in five minutes," said Hannah, disappearing into the bathroom.

I went straight down and lingered in the big dining hall, pretending to myself that this was where we were having breakfast. There were great big silver dishes on the sideboards; if I lifted the lids they'd probably be full of kidneys and mushrooms and stuff. In a minute, a very old maidservant would come in and curtsy. "Just the smoked haddock for me this morning, Lucinda," I'd say.

"Morning, dear!" Gran said, putting her head round the door. "Talking to yourself?"

I felt myself go red. "Just humming," I said.

After breakfast in Gran's kitchen (cereal – the same type as we have at home) Hannah and I were allowed to look round the castle. I was a bit disappointed when Gramps said we could go anywhere we liked.

"Isn't there just one room we mustn't go in? A little room upstairs that only you have the key to?" I asked.

He laughed. "What – with a mad bear chained up inside?"

"Or a dreadful ghoul rattling its chains?" I asked eagerly.

He shook his head and twiddled his moustache. "You can go wherever you like, my dears."

We went all over, looking in all the rooms. Some were open to the public and fully furnished just as if people were living in them, but those that weren't open had their curtains pulled and all the furniture covered with big white dustsheets. Dead creepy, those were.

"I've been in all these before," Hannah complained after about twelve rooms, casting longing glances out of the windows.

"You go and look for birds if you like, then," I said straight away. I was dying to get on and look on my own; she wasn't doing it properly. If I said something like, "There's a strange noise outside on the drive! Is it the clatter of the hoofs of long-dead horses drawing a funeral carriage?" she'd say, "Of course it isn't, it's the milkman."

She dived off to get her binoculars and reference books and I carried on on my own, making careful notes. For instance: *Room 6, ground floor. Curtains seem to move of their own accord. Suspect ghostly presence.*

Eventually I made my way back to the dining room and studied the walls minutely, counting backwards and forwards to make sure each had the same number of panels up and down.

I tapped to test whether any of them would swing round and reveal a secret hidden tunnel, or maybe a secret room with a skeleton propped up reading a Bible.

I checked I had my torch and a small reserve of chocolate, just in case I was gone for some time. The torch was OK, but I'd absent-mindedly eaten the chocolate while I'd been looking round. I just had to hope that I wouldn't be gone long.

I slid my fingers up and down the carved bits and pushed in all the corners. I'd just about finished the second wall and was down on all fours, tapping along the skirting board behind one of the big sideboards, when Gran came in.

I thought perhaps she might just be passing through and wouldn't spot me, so I sort of froze to the spot, but then she started fiddling about with the flower arrangements and I knew I'd have to come out.

I gave a nervous cough, crawled further along and stood up.

"There! That's done that!" I said.

She jumped backwards, her pearls rattling. "Bless my soul!" she said. "You gave me quite a turn! Whatever were you doing down there?"

I flourished the hanky that, luckily, Mum had put in my jeans pocket. "Just a spot of dusting," I said.

"Dusting?"

I shook out the hanky and hoped that Gran wouldn't notice that no dust came off. "Mum said I had to be helpful," I explained in a goody-goody voice. "I was just doing my bit."

"Oh, there's really no need!" she said. "The whole place gets a spring clean when we close. They send an army of cleaning people in."

"Oh, well," I said modestly. "I expect every little helps."

She showed no inclination to leave, so I went outside and wrote in my notebook, *Strong possibility of secret room behind panelling*

in dining room. Was stopped by Authorities from
investigating further.

After we'd eaten a sandwich lunch,
Hannah set off birdwatching again (she'd
seen seventeen different species that
morning, she said) and I set off counting
windows round the castle. In books, what
happens is that on a careful count along the
ground floor, there always turn out to be
more windows than there are rooms. This
leads to the discovery of a small room with a
Dreadful Secret inside. Or a treasure. I didn't
much mind which it was; I thought either
would be enough to get me on television –
just on *Children's Newsday* or something,
enough to make me fairly famous.

I drew up a rough plan of each exterior wall
and marked all the windows off, then I went
inside and started counting rooms. The
trouble was, in books there's just one window
to each room so you know where you are, but
in Murdo Castle some rooms had one
window, others had two, three or even four,

and it all got so awful and complicated that I got angry, tore the page right out and jumped on it. Then I remembered about litter in the grounds so tore it into a hundred pieces and put it in a litter bin.

Fed up, and nibbling a fraction of (rather fluffy) chocolate I'd found in my jacket pocket, I wandered off to the formal garden, which consisted of clipped box hedges, neatly trimmed plants and – I peered down a small avenue – some interesting-looking statues.

I walked down among them. Here, of course, would be someone wicked in the Murdo family who'd been cursed and turned to stone by a witch. At the stroke of midnight each New Year's Eve he would be allowed one hour of freedom.

Suddenly, further down the statue avenue, a shape moved. My stomach lurched with fright. Maybe … maybe this year he'd come alive ahead of schedule...

Nervously, hiding behind each statue along the way, I made my way to the bottom, where the pond was. If this wicked Murdo asked me to carry out some mission for him I'd say I was just a mortal child, didn't even live here and my mum was expecting me home on Friday.

Something moved again. I fled for a bush as – *the gardener* came out from behind a hedge, wheeling a barrow!

"Afternoon, dear," he said. "Nice day it's turned out!"

"Very nice," I said politely.

As he passed the pond I noticed, to my further disgust, that he had a reflection.

Chapter Six

"I think I've seen something rare," Hannah said the next morning, just as we were finishing breakfast in the kitchen.

"You're always saying that," I said, trying to push my bulb of garlic up my jumper sleeve. The sleeve had gone baggy so it kept falling down.

"No, I mean it this time. Something very rare. A White's thrush."

"Well," I said, "it doesn't sound very rare – not like a lesser-spotted pyewacket or something like that."

"Never heard of it."

"Said it was rare!" I said triumphantly. "Here, never mind white thrushes – you haven't seen any huge black ravens, have you? Or –" a thought suddenly struck me – "any bats? Especially any bats which seem to transform themselves into vampires as they land."

"Strangely enough, I haven't," said Hannah. She picked up her wellies from beside the back door. "It's your turn to wash up, isn't it? I'm going to have to spend a good lot of time in the wood today."

"Well, don't let me stop you," I said. "I'm going to be busy hunting for mirrors."

She screwed up her face. "What for?"

"Well, in this book I read…" But before I'd got more than two sentences into the story, she'd disappeared quicker than a vampire when the sun comes up.

Gran came back in. She'd been in the hall, setting out the brochures for that day's visitors.

"Hannah gone already?" she asked.

"Gone very-rare-bird spotting," I said, clearing away the dishes.

"Don't worry about those," Gran said. "I'll do them after we've had our elevenses. You go off and explore if you like."

I put the dishes down on the draining board and as I did so the bulb of garlic fell out of my sleeve and rolled across the floor.

Gran stared as it reached her feet.

"Whatever's that you've dropped?" she

asked. I went to pounce, but she'd already got her hand on it. "Garlic! Whatever are you carrying garlic around for?"

I thought quickly. "My ... er ... mum sent it for you," I said. Well, she had, in a roundabout sort of way.

"Sent it for *me*?" Gran asked, more and more puzzled.

"She thought you might need it. For cooking," I said. "She thought it might be rare in this part of the country."

"Did she really," Gran said faintly. "How kind."

She put it on the side, from where, later, it would no doubt join the flowers in the dustbin. So I was not only without a stake to drive through a vampire's heart, but I didn't have any garlic either. I just had to hope I didn't meet Dracula, that was all.

"Er, as the public are around today, d'you think I could possibly explore upstairs – in the attic?" I asked tentatively.

"I should think so," Gran said. "Although

it's in a terrible mess, and there's no electric light."

"I've got a torch," I said eagerly. "And I'll be very careful. Er, are there any mirrors up there?"

"There might be," said Gran. "I really don't know. There could be anything."

Great, I thought.

The staircase which led up to the attic was narrow and winding and far away from the touristy parts of the house. I checked that my torch was working and up I went, my heart thumping like mad.

The door at the top was stuck at first and I had to give it a great heave, but when I eventually got in I found I could do without the torch – there was just enough light coming in from the little dormer windows.

I glanced around quickly – no skeletons, but heaps of interesting junk. Old chairs, mostly, and packing cases and piles of magazines and water tanks and old bits of farming equipment.

My careful, trained eye ran over everything and I gave a little cry of glee – a rocking chair! I'd read a book about a haunted rocking chair that, whenever terrible bad luck was going to befall the house, spookily began to rock all on its own.

Squeezing between piles of yellow newspapers, I gave the rocking chair a little push to start it off. It tipped forwards, backwards, then stopped. I gave it another, heftier push and it did the same again. I tried once more and then gave up. In my notebook I wrote, *Spooky old rocking chair discovered. By careful experiment I have concluded that it does not want to rock on its own, therefore no terrible bad luck is going to befall Murdo Castle in the near future.*

I moved on. There was nothing very exciting after all. No carved wooden rocking horses or ventriloquists' dummies waiting to come alive, or big beautiful doll's houses. No doll's houses at all, actually, so I couldn't even pretend to myself that one was haunted by a family of people who'd been shrunk by a magician. (I'd read that book last year.)

But tiptoeing over to the window past an armchair that had its stuffing coming out, at last I found what I'd been looking for – a mirror!

I gave it careful, detective-like consideration. It was very old, some sort of rare ebony wood, I thought. It was smallish, square and on a stand. I'd been hoping for a tall one that stood on the floor, a full-length one that a person could walk through, but this would obviously have to do. I'd just have to go through bit by bit; hand first, then arm, then the rest of me. Suppose some of the bits got stuck in the wrong time zone, though? Suppose my toes were in 1993 but the rest of me was in 1793? I hesitated, then thought that I'd just have to worry about that when it happened.

I held up the mirror. What should happen next? In the book, it went all misty and the girl felt herself unaccountably, spookily, drawn in.

I squeezed up my eyes so that everything did go misty; got that bit right. Then I tried to push my hand through to the other time zone.

Nothing happened. Maybe I ought to *say* something. What, though? In the books they never had to.

"Magic mirror, magic mirror," I intoned, feeling daft. "Magic mirror, let me through!"

It was no good. I felt silly – as if I were playing the wolf in "The Three Little Pigs".

I pushed harder, screwed my eyes up tighter – and the mirror fell out of my hand and crashed on the floorboards. It broke into little bits, the plastic back came off, and so did the sticky label which said: *Shaving mirror. Made in Taiwan.*

Well, of all the rotten fakes. And then I remembered something else – you got seven years' bad luck from a broken mirror!

I glanced nervously at the rocking chair. It hadn't started moving, but perhaps I ought to get out quickly, before it did. Eyes carefully averted from the chair, I grabbed my torch and bolted back down the stairs.

Chapter Seven

"Can I use the library, Gramps?" Hannah asked the next morning when we were up, dressed and outside. "I'll be very quiet. I won't get in the way of any visitors."

Gramps was out at the front of the castle, putting up the car park signs. "Course you can, ducks," he said.

"I just want to see if I can find any record of this really rare bird I think I've seen."

I thought quickly. "Can I use the library, too?" I asked. "I want to see if I can find any record of vampires."

"Vampires?" Gramps said, startled.

"Vampire bats," Hannah broke in quickly.

"Yes, vampire bats. Most interesting," I said.

"Well, you two help yourselves," Gramps said. "It'll be good to see all those books being used by someone."

We went off to get our notebooks. As soon as Hannah had said "library", you see, I'd realized – that was where the secret room would be. All I had to do was remove a certain book from a certain shelf and this would trigger a switch so that a whole wall of books would swing round to reveal the secret room that I hadn't found by counting along the windows outside.

As we came down the stairs into the hall Gran was on the phone. "It's your mum!" she called to me, then carried on chatting. "Yes, she's fine," she said. "And the two of them haven't been any trouble at all – in fact I hardly see them... Yes, Hannah's dad will collect them on Friday. Oh, and by the way, Mrs Davies, thank you so much for the flowers." I made a lunge for the phone, but she carried on: "And the garlic, of course. Most thoughtful."

Gran, smiling, handed the phone over to me.

"What on earth did she mean – *garlic*?" Mum said.

I smiled glassily at Gran. "Don't know."

"Is she *all right*?"

"Can't say really," I muttered, while Gran

and Hannah admired some stained glass with a bird on it in the door.

"Is she very old, Amy? Just say yes or no."

"Mmm," I said.

"A bit dotty, I suppose, and you can't talk about it because she's around. How are you, anyway?"

"Fine," I said.

"Having a good time?"

"Great!"

"Well, I just thought I'd check. See you Friday, then. Oh, and Amy?"

"Yes?"

"If she really is dotty, make sure she doesn't leave the cooker on all night or start a fire or anything."

"OK," I said, smiling even more glassily at Gran.

The tourists had been let in by the time we got to the library. A few of them stared at us as, rustling our notebooks importantly, we marched in and made ourselves at home.

Most of the books were so huge and hefty

that you couldn't even pick them off the shelves. Not that you'd have wanted to – they looked deadly dull. There was a reference section, though, which had encyclopaedias and things.

Hannah found the birds and nature bit. I just moved round taking likely-looking volumes off the shelves. It would have been helpful if I could have found something called *This Is the One That Will Reveal the Secret Passage*, but I couldn't.

Instead they had titles like *Land and Ownership in the Seventeenth Century*, *Our Heritage Explained* and *A Pastoral Land Remembered*. Not a whiff of a spook.

I did find one called *Local Myths and Legends* that was quite interesting, but after an hour of not finding anything about Murdo ghosts or a secret passage I started to get fed up. Hannah kept making little squeaks and noises of excitement, although when I looked over her shoulder all I could see was pictures of bits of birds – birds' wings and beaks and tails, hundreds of them listed in a sort of catalogue.

"Bor–ing!" I said. "How on earth can you get interested in pictures of birds' bottoms?"

She gave another squeak and scribbled something in her notebook. "It *is*, I'm sure it is!" she muttered to herself.

Two Americans came in. I knew they were Americans because he had a big tartan golfing cap on and she was wearing a fur coat.

"Glorious place you have here!" he said.

I smiled graciously as if I personally owned Murdo Castle.

"Is it haunted?" the woman asked.

I smiled more warmly; here was a woman after my own heart.

"Naturally," I said.

She nudged her husband. "Didn't I tell you? These places are always haunted." She came closer. "Can you tell me about any ghosts, honey?"

"Sure!" I said. "I mean, I haven't actually

seen any here yet but, well, as you said, places like this always have them, don't they? I've made a study of them." I coughed discreetly. "I'm hoping to be on television quite soon. I'm a bit of an authority, actually, so it's lucky you asked. You get the various types of spook. There's the—"

"And is your friend studying them also?" the man interrupted, nodding towards Hannah.

I shook my head dismissively. "Oh, no! All she's interested in is birds."

"Birds!" the woman said. "Off you go, Sam, and talk to that young lady, while I find out about the ghosts." She edged closer to me. "Sam's keen on birds, too. At home he's gone for days on end."

While Sam started chatting to Hannah, I started telling the woman about all the spooks I could think of. I went through vampires and monsters and dead knights in armour and wailing ghosts, witches and wizards – every ghoulish thing I'd ever read about, in fact, while she stood there, open mouthed. After those I went on to time zones, magic mirrors and secret rooms where walled-up skeletons could be found, and by the time I'd finished, Hannah and Mr American had moved across the library and were standing by one of the big windows, looking towards the wood and talking earnestly.

"Well, that's been *so* interesting," the woman said to me. "I'm going to start hunting straight away. Come on, Sam!" she called. "I want to go into the dining hall and tap some panelling!"

"Do you know, this young lady thinks she's seen a White's thrush?" Sam said.

"That's all very well, Sam, but you can do your birds at home. While we're in England we've got to do ghosts."

They went off in the direction of the dining hall.

"Fancy her being interested in daft old ghosts," Hannah said when they'd gone.

"Fancy him being interested in daft old birds," I replied.

It was nearly lunch time by then, so Hannah and I went back to the kitchen to get a sandwich. As I munched on my cheese and pickle I wrote, *Investigated library, looking for secret revolving wall to be triggered by removing a book. Not yet found. Obviously extremely well hidden.*

When Gramps came in I asked him if there was any record of treasure being lost in the castle.

"Not that I know of, ducks," he said, twiddling. "Though I once lost fifty pence – it had rolled under the fridge. Does that count?"

I smiled politely.

"I've been looking in the books," Hannah said, "but they don't come up any further than 1910. I can't find out for sure...
I suppose you wouldn't know if a White's thrush has been spotted in the wood recently?"

I gave an exaggerated screech of boredom. "Oh, not that old bird again, Hannah. Talk about yawn!"

The next day I was going to wish I hadn't said that.

Chapter Eight

The next morning, waking up unsquashed again, I had a new thought. There was one thing I hadn't looked at properly in the castle – portraits of Murdo ancestors. You see, I'd read this book only a few months ago about a family in which there'd been a really wicked uncle. He'd died, and all the people who didn't like him had been very pleased and relieved, until they'd noticed that in the big oil painting of Uncle that hung over the mantelpiece the eyes now came alive and strangely and spookily followed them round the room. This made them all get panicky and start killing themselves. Not deliberately, but because they were so worried that they started getting careless and falling down the stairs and all that.

Well, there were loads of portraits going back through the centuries in Murdo Castle, so I reckoned that there must have been a wicked uncle (or maybe even a wicked aunty) at some time, and why shouldn't their eyes come alive, too.

After breakfast, and once Hannah had gone out to bird-watch, I decided to draw up a proper plan of the castle, allocating two rooms to a page so I could note down the names of the portraits in each. That would be very efficient and businesslike, I thought. Besides, I wanted to use as many pages in my notebook as possible – Hannah had practically finished hers.

I started on the dining hall. There were seven portraits in there, all really ugly people with curly wigs and sneery looks on their faces. They could easily have been wicked uncles and aunties, they looked just the type.

I carefully wrote down everyone's names from the little brass plaques under the portraits, then studied their eyes. Wicked eyes, piggy eyes, yes. But were they *moving* wicked piggy eyes?

I was tiptoeing backwards and forwards across the room, dodging in between the furniture, staring at the portraits and trying to decide whether or not the eyes were following me, when suddenly my attention was caught by movement and noise outside.

I knew the public weren't in that day, so why had three black cars, two vans and a huge green lorry thing pulled up on the drive? Also, why were important-looking people with clipboards getting out of the cars, why was "Outside Broadcast" written on the lorry and why – I gave a scream – was there a television camera being wheeled out of the back of one of the vans?

As I dropped everything and ran for the door, I wondered how they'd heard about me and my spook investigations. Perhaps someone had seen my notebook or perhaps (it was Hallowe'en soon) they were going to stage some sort of "Night in Haunted Castle" stunt.

I charged out of the front door – straight into cameras, two arc lights and reels of cable.

"Ah! Here she is!" a tall woman with a clipboard said, and everyone looked round.

"You're the clever young lady we want!"

They *had* heard about me! I tried to look smilingly modest as a man with some sort of tape recorder joined her.

"Very observant of you," he said. "Have you always been interested in—"

"In spooks and mysteries?" I said eagerly. "Yes. Ever since I could read I—"

"In birds, I was going to say," the man said.

I stared at him, dumbstruck.

"Apparently this is the first spotting in this area for twenty-eight years. The White's thrush is hardly ever seen now. Everyone's terribly excited."

"I ... I..."

"An American chap phoned us with the news yesterday. We got on to the local ornithologists and someone came down at dawn and verified it. We've just now got your grandparents' permission to start filming."

"Well done!" the woman said, patting my shoulder as more people gathered round.

"We'll be interviewing you for local television later, but right now perhaps you could take me to where you first saw the bird."

"I ... but..." I stuttered. Oh, I was terribly tempted. I really had to struggle with my conscience – but I knew I'd never get away with it. "I ... it's not me you want. It was my friend who saw the bird," I said miserably. "My friend Hannah."

"Oh, I see," the woman said. She took her hand off my shoulder. "And, well, are you interested in birds, too, er...?"

"Amy," I said. I crossed my fingers. "Oh, yes, I love them. Terribly interested in ... er ... ornifillogy and white thrushes and things."

"Quite," the woman said. "And now do you think you could go and get Hannah for us?"

I ran off towards the woods, thumping over the grass and yelling excitedly, and was met by a cross-looking Hannah just coming out of the trees.

"For goodness' sake," she said. "You've just

sent every bird in there flying for cover. Don't you know better than to rush about bird sanctuaries yelling your head off?"

"I hope you're not going to be bad-tempered like that when you're being interviewed on television about your thrush!" I said, hopping up and down on the spot with excitement.

"What? What're you talking about?"

I put my arm through hers and dragged her along. "You'll never guess. It's the television! They've come to interview you about that old white thrush..."

"White's thrush?"

"Whatever it's called and ... well ... we *are* best friends, aren't we?"

"Mmm," she said, looking flustered.

"Well, as we're such best friends, d'you think you could pretend that I'm interested in birds, too..."

"What!"

When we got back it was all happening. Gramps and Gran had appeared with coffee for the crew, lights were being set up for the first interview, and a message had gone back to base that an aerial view of the wood was wanted, so would they please send a helicopter over with a cameraman on board.

As far as I was concerned, all was not lost. The woman said that I could appear in the background with Hannah's binoculars round my neck, looking as if I was waiting for her to join me for more bird-spotting.

That was OK, of course, that was very nice, but it was also disappointing. I wasn't going to be famous. I was just a bit of background.

And then, *then* – while we were waiting for them to start filming by the front door "because the stained glass will look pretty in the background" – I had a thought. A very clever, very spook-detective-like thought. I took another, closer, look at the stained glass, and disappeared into the library. You see, when I'd been hoping for walls to swing back the day before and I'd looked through *Local*

Myths and Legends, I'd seen something that in view of all this thrush business *could* be very important. I had to find the book again, because I had the strangest feeling. Almost a spooky feeling...

Five minutes later, the book clutched in my hand, I went back outside and approached the clipboard woman.

"Excuse me!" I said. She was doing something important with some sort of measuring device. "I've got something that might interest you."

"If it could wait until later," she began.

"But just listen," I said.

"I really haven't got time, dear."

A few of them were listening, though, so I read out loudly: "There is a legend, connected with Murdo Castle, concerning the White's thrush, which has been spotted in this country fewer than thirty times, usually in the vicinity of the Castle. Legend has it that the appearance of this rare and beautiful bird signals a great rise in prosperity, not only for the owners of Murdo Castle, but one that will be reflected in the country as a whole. The legend seems to have appealed to the Victorians, who celebrated the appearance of the bird by depicting it on a panel of stained glass. This can still be seen in the doorway to Murdo Castle."

When I'd finished reading, I took two steps back and pointed dramatically to the bird panel in the door. "And there it is!" I said.

Everyone gaped, everyone gasped, everyone rushed to get a better look. "Ooh, how interesting!" they said, "Well spotted!" and "Yes, it all adds up." Even the woman with the clipboard said it was most perceptive of me.

They let me be in the whole thing after that. Of course, I wasn't quite as important as Hannah, but very nearly. And as I said to her on the way home, "I told you I was going to be on television. I said I'd be famous."

"If it wasn't for me and my thrush you wouldn't be," she said. And, well, I let her get away with that because I wanted to be invited back to the castle again. I'd just remembered, you see, I hadn't even *started* on werewolves...

JACKSON'S JUNIORS

Vivian French

When twins Chris and Rosie set off for their first day at Jackson's Juniors, they hatch a brilliant plan: Chris will pretend that he can't speak and Rosie that she can't hear. The plan doesn't work out quite as planned, but it makes for a day that is often surprising, sometimes alarming and always eventful!

THE MYSTERY OF THE RUGGLESMOOR DINOSAUR

Alison Leonard

Danny and Lally are staying with their aunt while their mother is having a baby. The two children are adopted and worry about losing their place in their parents' affections. Then, with the arrival of a strange man, Hugo Byng, searching for dinosaur clues, Danny and Lally find themselves up to their eyes in a mysterious and thrilling adventure!

"A good old-fashioned adventure story for the Nineties." *The Sunday Telegraph*